*Dedicated to Mr. Cheung**
the nicest Chinese man in Holland,
who can sing beautifully!

*Pronounced: Tsjoong

Never a dull moment with King Bobble!

Eerste druk, maart 2012
Tweede druk, april 2013

Copyright © 2012 Text by Marianne Busser and Ron Schröder
and The House of Books, Vianen/Antwerp
Copyright © 2012 Illustrations by Dagmar Stam
and The House of Books, Vianen/Antwerp

Translation by Joan Edith Roberts
Book design by Petra Gerritsen, www.spletters.nl
ISBN 978 90 443 3422 7
NUR 277
D/2012/8899/72

www.mariannebusser-ronschroder.info
www.thehouseofbooks.com

Marianne Busser & Ron Schröder

Royal Dutch Bedtime Stories

Illustrated by Dagmar Stam

the house of books

An introduction

King Bobble has a large head. The Queen also has a large head.
That is why they wear car tyres instead of a crown. Three times
the King has won the Giant Head Competition.
This is a pity for the Queen as she has only come second place.
But luckily she is very proud of the three silver trophies the
King received as his prize.
They live together in their pretty palace and they have a lot of
fun.
But now the time has come for them to visit a few famous
towns in their beautiful country. For surely there is not a nicer
country than Holland?

Contents

Two Pairs of Clogs
and a Handy Windmill

King Bobble wants new shoes. And the Queen also wants new shoes.
'Would you like sandals or flip-flops?' the footman asks them. 'Or maybe a pair of boots?'
'No,' replies the Queen. 'We would like something special.'
The footman thinks for a moment. 'What would you say to clogs?'
'Oh,' says the Queen. 'Is this something new?'
'Oh no,' replies the footman. 'Clogs have existed for close to 800 years.'
So off they go to the clog maker.
'What can I do for you?' asks the clog maker.
'We would like a pair of clogs,' replies the Queen. 'And may we choose a colour?'
'Of course,' answers the clog maker. 'As long as it's yellow.'
A little later the King and Queen are proudly clunking around the shop in their yellow clogs.
'Shall we go home now?' asks the footman.
'No!' says the Queen. 'We want to practice in our new clogs.'

And so the three of them walk around the village. The footman in his shoes, and the King and Queen in their clogs.
'Look!' points King Bobble. 'A windmill! Let's have a look.'

'Good afternoon,' the miller greets them. 'Are you wearing new clogs? They look so clean and shiny!'

'We have just bought them,' the Queen proudly replies. 'But I would like to know why clogs are made of wood. Do you have any idea?'

The miller points to a ditch. 'If a clog falls into the water it will float. And that can be very handy.'

'Oh, my dear!' exclaims the Queen. 'That is certainly handy, because we will be able to walk on the water!'

And before the miller can say anything, they run to the ditch.

Then the miller and the footman hear a loud splash.

'Incredible,' says the footman. 'Never a dull moment.'

And then both he and the miller run to the ditch.

First they drag the Queen out, and then the King. They stand on the grass, soaked trough.

'This is your fault,' the Queen accuses the miller. 'You told us that clogs float!'

'Yes, clogs do,' replies the miller. 'But not when you are wearing them!'

'You should have told us so!' she says. 'Now we are soaking wet. How can we get into the coach looking like this?'

'Come with me,' the miller calmly replies. 'I have some spare clothes in the windmill, which you can wear. We will hang your wet clothes on the sails of the windmill. They will dry in no time at all. Quite nifty, eh?'

And so it happened. The King and Queen sit inside the windmill dressed in blue overalls. Their clothes turn around on the sails of the windmill.

And the miller makes them some hot chocolate, because that is what they do in Holland when you fall into a ditch! ✤

Photos in Volendam and a Big Kiss from the Queen

King Bobble looks at photos. The Queen also looks at photos.
'Look at this one!' King Bobble says to the footman. 'What do you see in this photo?' The footman looks. 'A wardrobe.'
'Yes,' says the Queen. 'And what else do you see?'
'I am sorry,' mutters the footman. 'But I only see a wardrobe.'
'Yes,' the King says proudly. 'That is because it is a hiding-photo. We are inside that wardrobe. You never would have guessed that, right?'
'No,' replies the footman. 'I would not have thought of that.'
'Isn't it great?' exclaims the Queen. 'And what do you see in this photo?'
'A curtain,' replies the footman.
'Anything else?' asks the King.
'Nothing,' says the footman. 'Just a curtain.'

'Not just a curtain,' exclaims King Bobble. 'Because we are behind that curtain. Isn't that funny?'

'Very funny,' says the footman politely.

'I would like a lot more trick photos!' exclaims the Queen.

'Well…' says the footman. 'In that case I have a surprise for you. I know someone who can take very special photos.'

An hour later the King and the Queen arrive in Volendam.

'What a quaint town,' says King Bobble. 'The townspeople are wearing such beautiful clothes!'

'This is the Dutch national costume,' explains the footman. And with that he takes the King and Queen along to a photographers studio.

'How can I be of service?' asks the photographer.

'We would like to have our photograph taken,' says the King.

'In your own clothes, or in the Volendam costume?'

'The costume,' replies the Queen. 'Because we like special photos.'

The photographer nods. 'Then we will have a rummage.'

No sooner said than done, and the King and Queen are all dressed up in the Volendam costume. Then the photographer gets started. First the Queen sits on the King's

knee. And then the King sits on the Queen's knee. The photographer snaps away. For the final shot they are to kiss each other.

And then the Queen says: 'Our footman must also have a photo taken in Volendam costume!'

'That won't be necessary,' says the footman. 'I do not like photos that much.'

'But WE do!' insists the Queen.

With a groan and a moan, the footman gets changed. 'Could it be one of those hiding photos?' he asks.

'Absolutely!' exclaims King Bobble. He grabs a waste-paper basket and plants it over the footman's head.

'Shoot,' commands the Queen.

And so the footman is photographed as well.

'You can all get changed now,' says the photographer.

The footman does so at once.

'Oh no!' says the Queen. She bursts into tears. 'We have never had such splendid clothes!'

'Oh,' says the photographer, taken aback. 'Well, you know what? You can borrow them for a short while.'

'And my husband too?' the Queen asks shakily.

The photographer nods. 'Yes, him too!'

The Queen gives the photographer a big kiss.

Happy as can be they return to the palace in their carriage. ❖

A Picnic Basket and a Disobedient Cow

King Bobble goes cycling. And the Queen also goes cycling.
Together they cycle past fields, and everywhere they look they see cows.
 'Let's join the cows in the field for our picnic,' says the Queen.
They lean their bikes against a tree and take their picnic basket.
Then they open the gate and go into the field.
'Hello cows!' says the Queen cheerfully. She lays down the
cloth and opens up the picnic basket.
But then a cow heads toward them. One bite and the
first sandwich is gone. And then the second, and then the
third…
'Stop it at once, cow,' the Queen says in her strictest voice.
'That is very naughty!'
But the cow only wants to eat more sandwiches.
'I shall ride her,' announces King Bobble. 'Then
she won't be able to take our sandwiches.'
The King tries to mount the cow. But that is
pretty difficult.
'I shall give you a push,' says the Queen. She
gives his bottom an upward shove. And then the
King sits proudly on top of the cow.
'I will take a photo of you!' says the Queen.
'Done it,' she says. 'Now go and have a ride.'

But the cow will not move.

'She won't budge,' grumbles King Bobble.

'You must ask her,' says the Queen.

'Please walk, little cow,' the King says politely.

But no, the cow still does not move.

'She clearly does not understand you,' says the Queen. 'It is probably not a Dutch cow. Perhaps she speaks Spanish.'

And so the King commands: 'Cowo walko pleaso!' To no avail. Nor does the cow listen to German, French or even Chinese.

Suddenly the Queen has a brilliant idea. She takes a sandwich from the picnic basket and stands in front of the cow. 'Come on, cow,' she says. 'Look what a nice sandwich I've got!'

Suddenly the cow wants to walk. She moves forward quickly toward the Queen.

The Queen takes fright. 'Help me!' she screams. 'Help me!' and runs away as fast she can.

The cow starts to run in pursuit of the Queen.

The King bounces wildly up and down: 'Ow, ow,' he yells. 'My bum! Get me off!'

The Queen runs on, through the gate and out of the field. She slams the gate shut in the cow's face.

The cow stops at once.

But King Bobble is flung over the gate and lands with a thud right next to the Queen.

'Oh, darling,' says the Queen. 'How terrible. Are you hurt?'

'Yes,' moans King Bobble, teary-eyed.

'Maybe we will come across a pig,' says the Queen, trying to comfort the King. 'Then you can ride the pig.'

But the King does not want to ride again. Not on a cow, not on a pig and not even on his bicycle.

'Shall we go and have some pancakes?' asks the Queen. 'That way we will still have something nice to eat.'

That makes King Bobble laugh a bit, because pancakes… Well, they are just the ticket on such occasions, what! ❖

Feeding Pigeons on Dam Square and a Mucky Head

King Bobble is in Amsterdam. The Queen is also in Amsterdam.
'Look!' says the footman. He points out a large town square covered with pigeons. 'This is Dam Square.'
'What are all those pigeons doing there?' King Bobble asks.
'Well, they are hoping to find a tasty snack,' replies the footman.
'Oh,' says the Queen. 'What a shame we don't have anything for them.'
But then the footman takes two little bags out of his bag. 'This is corn,' he says. 'The gardener sent it along for you. Pigeons love corn.'
'That was kind of him,' the Queen says. She then looks at the fluttering birds. She finds them scary and doesn't dare feed them. Then she sees the King and she starts to laugh a bit. 'Stand still, my dear,' she says. 'There is a little bit of dust on your tyre. I shall remove it.'
The Queen gets behind the King and tries to tip all her corn into the middle of his tyre.
But she is too short.
The Queen whispers something into the footman's ear.

The footman shakes his head. 'No,' he says, quietly. 'I will not do that.'

'But I am not asking you to do it,' the Queen whispers. 'I am telling you to!'

'Well, okay,' says the footman. He sighs and empties the whole bag of corn into the middle of the King's tyre.

When the pigeons see the corn in the middle of the King's tyre, they start pecking at once.

'Ouch!' yells the startled King. 'Do not peck my head! It hurts!'

He quickly scatters corn onto the ground.

The pigeons start eating there.

'What a relief,' says King Bobble. 'I lost them.'

But when they are finished, the pigeons flutter straight to his head again.

'Go away!' screams the King.

'Those little dears are just hungry,' says the Queen.

Then the Queen sees a chip stand. 'Would you like some chips?' she asks the pigeons.

'I am sure they do,' the King says.

So the Queen quickly buys a bag of chips.

Then, with a startled look at the King, she says, 'My dear! Your tyre is suddenly white!'

'That is pigeon poo, Your Majesty,' says the footman.

'The pigeons have sat on the tyre and then they have, eh...'

'Whoops-a-daisy?' asks the Queen.

'No,' mutters the footman. 'Poops-a-daisy.'

'Yuck!' says the Queen. 'And you are the one to blame. You should never have put the corn into the King's tyre!'

'But you commanded me!' exclaims the footman.

'Nonsense,' replies the Queen. 'You are a grown-up, and you could have said NO.'

'Do I now have poo on my tyre?' asks King Bobble.

'Yes,' says the Queen. 'Those pigeons pooed on your head.'

'But that is horrid!' says a distressed King.

'Quite so,' says the Queen. 'But our footman will take you to a hotel. You will be able to wash it off there.'

'Right,' says the footman. 'Follow me. I see one already.'

A quarter of an hour later, they reappear.

'Clean as a whistle!' exclaims the King. 'And the hotel gave me one of their fine soaps!'

But then the Queen bursts into tears. 'I want a soap too!' she exclaims.

'Not possible,' replies King Bobble. 'Because you do not have poo on your head.'

And that is true. To get a fine soap you must first have the poo-experience! ♣

A Canal Tour
and Dry Pants

King Bobble sees a boat. The Queen also sees a boat. The boat is full of people.
'Brilliant!' exclaims the Queen. 'A canal tour. Shall we go and sail through
Amsterdam as well?'
The King shakes his head. 'No, I'd rather have an ice cream.'
'Nonsense,' says the Queen. 'You've already had an ice cream!'
'Yes,' says the King. 'But I want another.'
The Queen pretends not to hear. She says to the captain. 'Two tickets, please.'
'That will not be possible,' says the captain, 'the boat is full.'
'Well, in that case we shall sit on the roof,' says the Queen. 'Will you fetch us
two deck chairs? After all, it's not every day you have royalty on board.'
'True, true,' the captain mutters. And he leaves to fetch the chairs.

Soon afterwards, the King and Queen are seated on the roof.
'Isn't it lovely here?' says the Queen.
'I don't like it,' King Bobble complains. 'I am going to keep my eyes closed.'
The Queens nods. 'Alright, then I will tell you what there is to see.'
'Well, I am not going to listen,' he says. He puts his fingers into his ears.
But the boat is heading for a very low bridge.
'Duck!' the captain shouts. 'Duck or there will be an accident!'
'We will,' replies the Queen, and she instantly lies flat.

But the King sees nothing and hears nothing. He stays exactly as he is. And that is when it happens. The King's tyre collides with the bridge, and he topples headlong into the canal…

The captain stops the boat, and slowly reverses.

Curious, the Queen peers over the edge of the boat. And indeed there is the King in the canal. 'Are you alright, dearest?' she asks.

But the King hears nothing. He is just going for another dip.

Meanwhile a large audience has gathered.

'What on earth is he up to?' a man exclaims.

Someone else shouts, 'See if you can find my bike on the bottom!'

'Really, indeed,' says a posh lady. 'You should mind your manners, it happens to be a King in the canal!'

'And a fat one too!' shouts a construction worker. 'What an enormous splash!'

The captain hurls a life buoy in the King's direction.

'Just stay there for a moment, my dear,' the Queen exclaims. 'I will quickly take a photo of you.'

But the Queen isn't the only one taking photos. A whole batch of photographers has gathered at the scene.

'Smile!' says the Queen. 'Tomorrow you'll be in all the papers'.

But the King is not amused. He looks very angry.

'Cheer up!' says the Queen. 'We'll go and get some ice cream soon.'

'A pair of dry pants seems to be a better plan,' says the captain.

King Bobble couldn't agree more. ✤

Flying Potatoes and Two Special Presents

The King wants to make a present. The Queen also wants to make a present.

'I shall make a clay vase for our footman,' says the King.

'And I shall make a plate for our cook,' replies the Queen.

They get their bucket with clay.

A little later they are busy. The Queen makes a plate and the King a vase.

But it is not an easy task. The plate is not round and the vase looks like a thick cucumber.

They try everything: a cup, a saucer, an egg cup… But nothing looks good.

'How annoying,' says the Queen.

'I quit,' grumbles the King.

'I'm going to make something else.' He quickly rolls up a ball of clay. 'This is a flying potato,' he says. He throws it in the air. The potato hits the ceiling and stays put.

'That's funny,' says the Queen. 'I will try it too.'
Then there are two clay potatoes on the ceiling.

The footman enters. 'What on earth is going on?' he asks.
'We wanted to make presents,' says King Bobble. 'But they didn't turn out.
That's why we made two flying potatoes. Look.' He points to the ceiling.
'That is bad, isn't it?' says the footman.
'We are going to have to repaint the
ceiling if this goes on!'
Then suddenly the flying potatoes fall
to the ground. But there are no marks
on the ceiling.
'Good,' says the footman. 'Shall
we drive to Delft? There they can
teach you how it's really done. That
is where they make the beautiful blue
and white Dutch crockery.'
But King Bobble does not want to make
anything anymore. And he doesn't
want to learn anything. He asks,
'Can you also buy things
in Delft?'
'Indeed you can,' says the
footman. 'All kinds of
things.'
And that makes the
King want to go too.

After an hour or so they are at the shop. 'Wait at the door,' the King tells the footman. 'We are going to buy presents.'

The King buys a vase for the footman. And the Queen buys a Delft blue and white plate for the cook. They hide the presents in a bag, and soon they are driving home again.

When they get home, the Queen tells the footman, 'Please go into the kitchen. We will be there in a minute.'

'I've got a great idea,' says the Queen. 'Let's have a race, and whoever wins can give his or her present first.'

'Ready steady GO!' replies the King, and they dash up the hallway.

But suddenly everything goes wrong. With a loud *bang* they bump into each other. *Boom*! The beautiful presents fly into the air and land on the stone floor.

'Whoops!' says King Bobble. He picks up his present. 'It seems to be rattling a bit.'

'Mine too,' says the Queen, concerned. 'It could be broken.'

'Well,' says the King, 'we'll pretend that is how it's supposed to be.'

And with that they enter the kitchen.

'We have a gift for you,' says the Queen proudly. 'But you will have to put it together yourselves.'

'Is it a puzzle?' asks the footman.

'Yes,' says King Bobble. 'Exactly! If you put the pieces together it will make a vase.'

'And you can make a plate,' says the Queen to the cook.

The cook and the footman unwrap their presents.

'What a lot of pieces,' says the footman. 'This really is a very special gift.'

'Yes,' says the cook. 'It will be a lot of work to make a vase and a plate.'

'That's alright,' says the Queen. 'Because it isn't a lot of fun if the puzzle is too easy, is it?'

Luckily the cook and the footman agree. ✤

Going to the Cheese Market in Alkmaar and a Painful Bottom

King Bobble wants to go to the cheese market. And the Queen also wants to go to the cheese market.

So off they go to Alkmaar with the cook and the footman.

After an hour or so the footman announces, 'We have arrived.'

'Are you coming?' King Bobble asks the cook and the footman.

'No,' replies the footman. 'I don't like cheese.'

'I will stay here too,' mutters the cook.

'Alright,' says the Queen. 'We will see you later.'

She walks through the market with the King. What a sight to see. All around the market square there are piles of cheese. Men in white overalls carry them around on great wooden boards.

'What a great job,' says King Bobble.

Suddenly the Queen starts to laugh. 'May I ask you something?' she says to one of the cheese carriers. 'May our cook and footman carry some cheeses too?'

'But they would never want to,' the King exclaims.

'No,' says the Queen. 'But we can tease them a little, can't we?'

The Queen implores the cheese carriers. 'May we?'

'Oh, alright then,' the cheese carriers say.

The Queen walks to the coach and yells, 'Surprise! You may become cheese carriers!'

But the cook and the footman do not want to.

'Nonsense,' says the Queen. 'You must! You will never have another chance.'

A little later the cook and the footman are walking grumpily in white overalls carrying a board piled with cheeses.

'You are doing great!' exclaims King Bobble, proudly.

'Could they carry me too?' asks the Queen.

'No,' says one of the cheese carriers. 'Cheese carriers can only carry cheese.'

'Then I shall pretend that I am a cheese,' says the Queen. She jumps on top of the pile of cheeses. The cook and the footman are startled. Then they walk on while huffing and puffing. But suddenly the board breaks in two. The cheeses roll in every direction around the town square and the Queen lands with her bottom onto the cobblestones. She squeals with laughter as she sits amongst the remaining cheeses. People are running over from all directions to take a picture of the Queen.

'Are you alright, my dear?' asks King Bobble.

'Yes, I am fine,' says the Queen. 'Only my bottom hurts. It must be black and blue.'

'Shall I check?' asks the King.

'No,' whispers the Queen. 'Royal bottoms are a very private matter!'
The Queen sits down. 'Ouch,' she calls out.
'Sit on your tyre,' says the King.
But the Queen refuses. 'I feel undressed without the tyre on my head.'
One of the cheese carriers grabs a cheese and cuts out a hole. 'Put this cheese on your head, so you can sit on your tyre.'
'Can I have one too?' asks the King.
'No!' says the Queen. 'Because your bottom is quite fine.'
The King immediately drops down.
'But now it isn't!'
And the King also gets a cheese on his head.
'Now we are real big Dutch cheese,' he says proudly.
And that is the absolute truth! ✤

A Colouring Competition,
the Keukenhof Gardens
and a Funny Street-Organ

King Bobble is colouring a colouring page. The Queen is also colouring a colouring page.

They are doing their very best, because they want to win the colouring competition.

'What colour are tulips?' asks the King.

'Red,' answers the Queen.

'Oh dear,' mutters the King. 'I've just done a blue one.'

'That is quite silly, my dear,' says the Queen. 'Tulips are red, just like tomatoes and strawberries. Have you ever seen blue ones?'

'Tulips come in every colour,' explains the footman.

'Nonsense!' replies the Queen. 'They only exist in red.'

'What about yellow tulips?' asks the footman.

'Those are obviously not real tulips,' says the Queen. 'Otherwise they would have been red.'

The footman sighs deeply. 'Do you know what? Let's go to the Keukenhof Gardens. There are lots of tulips there. You can see for yourselves what colours tulips come in.'

'Which is red,' the Queen says.

'Yes,' says the footman grumpily. 'And yellow and blue and white and pink and a lot more colours.'

A short while later they enter the Keukenhof Gardens. They are amazed.
'You are right after all,' says the Queen to the footman. 'There are tulips in
lots of different colours. I will pick some.'
'That is not allowed,' says the footman. 'You can only look at the flowers
and take photographs. But we could buy a bunch later on.'
'Hush and listen,' says King Bobble. 'I hear music.'
'That is a street-organ,' says the footman. 'It is just around the corner.'
The King and Queen head over at once.
'This is great!' the Queen exclaims. 'Shall we dance?'

'Rather not,' says the
footman hastily. He steps
back nervously.
'I was inviting my
husband,' says the Queen.
'I was not planning to
dance with you!'

The King and the Queen
twirl around. 'This is my
very best dance,' says the
Queen.
'Yes,' agrees the King,
proudly. 'I am a natural,
right?'
'I think it is because of
the clogs,' says the Queen.
'That's why I can't feel
you treading on my
toes.'
And with that they
give each other a
quick kiss.
'When we get home, I will do
some more colouring,' says the Queen. 'Maybe we
will win a street-organ!' she exclaims. 'Then we can dance every day!'
But the King would rather win a pancake booth. Dancing is alright, but
only now and then… ❖

A Huge Snowman and a Footman Wearing a Bucket on his Head

King Bobble has fallen sixteen times. And the Queen seventeen times already. But now they have had enough. 'I'm never skating here again,' says the Queen. 'The ice is far too slippery. They should have grit it better.' And so they walk home together.

'Are you back already?' asks the surprised footman.

'Yes,' says the King. 'It wasn't any fun. We're going to make a snowman now.' They make an immediate start. Firstly they roll a great snowball, and then they place a smaller one on top. They get a carrot for a nose, and use stones for the eyes and mouth. They get an old scarf, a broom and a car tyre from their shed for the snowman. And now he is finished!

'What shall we do next?' the Queen asks the footman.

'Throwing snowballs might be a good idea,' says the footman.

Right away King Bobble makes a snowball and throws it into the air. 'I do not like it,' he grumbles.

'Well, you need to make it more exciting,' says the footman. 'You should try to hit a target.'

The King throws a snowball at a tree. 'Boring,' he says.

'Just a minute,' shouts the Queen. She runs inside and returns with a small red bucket. 'You stand over there,' she tells the footman. 'And then you put the bucket on your head and close your eyes.'

'And what then?' asks the footman.

'That's a surprise,' says the Queen.

'I'm not sure if I will like this,' mutters the footman.

'Surely,' says the Queen, 'it is very exciting. And you said yourself that we should throw snowballs.'

'True,' says the footman. And he sighs and puts the red bucket on his head.

'And now we are going to try to knock it off,' says the Queen. She throws a snowball at the bucket first. 'Nearly,' she exclaims.

'That was my ear,' says the footman. And next it's the King's turn to aim. His snowball hits the footman right on the nose.

The footman wipes the snow off his face. 'I quit,' he says.
'Spoilsport,' says the Queen.
'Yes,' says the King. 'It's fun and you could get used to it.'
'Okay, just for a bit then,' the footman gives in.

They hurl one snowball after the other in the direction of
the red bucket. Finally it falls to the ground.
'I am the winner!' yells King Bobble, proudly.
'No, I am!' screams the Queen.
'Stop,' says the footman. 'You are not going
to argue.'
'Anyway, what's the prize?' asks the Queen.
'The winner gets sprouts for dinner,' says the
footman. And he walks away with big steps.
'In that case you win, my dear,' the Queen
quickly says. 'I am thrilled for you!'
But King Bobble is not happy. If there
is one thing he doesn't like, it's got to
be sprouts. But unfortunately, nothing
can be done about it. After all he really
did win! ❖

A Visit to the Rijksmuseum and a Genuine Bobble in the Toilet

King Bobble wants to paint. And the Queen also wants to paint.

'But what shall we paint?' asks the King. 'An apple or a mushroom?'

'I've got a better idea,' says the Queen. 'You'll paint me and I'll paint you.'

The King likes this idea.

A short while later they call out, 'Finished!'

The footman comes to have a look. 'I am curious,' he says.

He looks at the paintings. 'Well done!' he says. 'Such amusing pigs!'

'Pigs?' says the Queen angrily. 'That's us! How dare you say that? Go back to the corridor and then come back in again.'

The footman blushes and walks to the corridor, and then re-enters. 'I am curious,' he says again.

He looks at the paintings. 'Well done!' he says. 'I can see right away that it's you! These could even be photographs.'

'That's more like it,' says King Bobble, satisfied. 'And now we are going outside. Where shall we go to?'

'Let's go to the Rijksmuseum,' says the footman. 'They have the most beautiful paintings in the whole world.'

'Is our work there?' asks the Queen.

The footman shakes his head.

'Then we shall take our paintings with us,' says the King.

And so they go to the Rijksmuseum in Amsterdam with their paintings.

'Good afternoon,' says the footman to the man at the museum.
'We have come to look at the paintings.'

'And to bring you some,' says the Queen, proudly. 'Just look!'

'What amusing pigs,' says the man at the museum.

'I do beg your pardon!' says the footman. 'These happen to be portraits of the King and Queen themselves.'

The man is taken aback. 'As if I didn't know that,' he quickly says.

'I thought I'd make a joke. I always say: A day without a laugh, is like curly kale without the sausage.'

'So you do like them?' asks the Queen.

The man at the museum nods. 'They're lovely.'

'Then we shall hang them at once,' says King Bobble. He takes two nails and a hammer from his back pocket.

'Well...' says the man at the museum, who is taken aback,
'I would not do that. Your paintings are just too good for a museum. They should be in a place where they can be quietly admired. Do you have space available in your toilet at home?'

'Good idea!' agrees the Queen. 'We will hang them together and write below it: THE KING AND THE QUEEN.'

'FOR WHEN YOU'VE BEEN!' rhymes King Bobble, falling about laughing.

Then they look at all the other paintings in the museum.

'These are such good colourings,' says the Queen. 'Did that big one over there win a prize?'

'That painting is called The Nightwatch,' says the footman. 'It was painted by Rembrandt and it is the most famous painting in Holland.'

'Why isn't it in the toilet, then?' asks the Queen, surprised.
'Only the most, most excellent paintings are hung in a
toilet,' says the man at the museum.
'I get it!' says the King. 'Not everyone can paint as well
as we. A real Rembrandt belongs in a museum and a
real Bobble in the toilet. There ought to be a difference
after all!'
And even the footman couldn't agree more. ♣

Marianne Busser and Ron Schröder are married and have written well over three hundred books and over one thousand songs together. They have also worked on the television show *Sesame Street*, created teaching methods for children and written articles for a variety of children's magazines.

www.mariannebusser-ronschroder.info